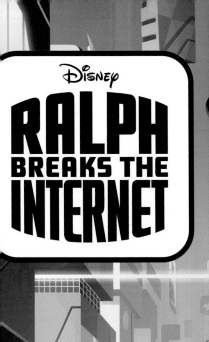

KT-423-663

# DISNEY

# RALPH BREAKS THE INTERNET

Autumn
Publishing

# Autumn
## Publishing

Published in 2018
by Igloo Books Ltd
Cottage Farm
Sywell
NN6 0BJ
www.igloobooks.com

© 2018 Disney Enterprises, Inc. All rights reserved.

No part of this publication may be
reproduced or transmitted in any form or by any means,
electronic, or mechanical, including photocopying, recording,
or by any information storage and retrieval system,
without permission in writing from the publisher.

GUA009 0918
2 4 6 8 10 9 7 5 3 1
ISBN 978-1-78905-184-1

Printed and manufactured in China

**This book belongs to:**

...........................................................................

Wreck-It Ralph and Vanellope were the best of friends. Ralph was the bad guy in *Fix-It Felix, Jr.* and Vanellope was the best racer in *Sugar Rush*. Every day, after Litwak's Arcade closed, the pair of them would hang out, play games and tell bad jokes. Their lives were practically perfect.

One day, a new plug-in for something called Wi-Fi appeared. Wi-Fi was a way to connect to the Internet. Not everyone was a fan. "The Internet is nothing to laugh at. It is new and it is different," said Surge Protector. "Therefore, we should fear it. So, keep out!"

Vanellope was disappointed they weren't allowed to go into the Internet. "A new racing game would have been cool," she told Ralph.

The next day, a young girl called Swati was playing *Sugar Rush*, but she pulled at the steering wheel so hard that it broke off in her hands! "I'm real sorry," she said to Mr. Litwak.

"It's okay," replied Mr. Litwak. "I think I can get it back on there pretty easy." When he tried, it snapped in two! "I'd order a new part," continued Mr. Litwak, "but the company that made *Sugar Rush* went out of business years ago."

Just then, one of the children told him a *Sugar Rush* wheel was for sale on eBay. It was far too expensive. Mr. Litwak decided he would have to unplug the game.

With Vanellope now homeless, Ralph took her to live in *Fix-It Felix, Jr.*. He tried to make her comfortable, but Vanellope felt lost. "I loved my game," she said. "If I'm not a racer anymore, who am I?"

Ralph didn't like seeing his best friend upset and left her to be alone, wondering how he could help.

After talking with Felix, Ralph remembered the steering wheel for sale on eBay. A plan popped into his head and he ran back to Vanellope. "Hey, kid," he said. "We're going to the Internet!"

Ralph and Vanellope snuck past Surge Protector and entered the Wi-Fi plug. The first stop was a large empty space – the router.

But Vanellope thought they were already in the Internet. "I have to admit, I'm underwhelmed," she said

Just then, Mr. Litwak logged onto the Internet and an avatar of him appeared and floated through the router.

"Come on, Ralph," said Vanellope. "Let's follow him!"

As the two stepped forward, they were enclosed in capsules and launched into the Internet.

"Ralph, isn't this great?" asked Vanellope.

"No, it is not!" replied Ralph, screaming.

Vanellope and Ralph landed slap bang in the middle of the Internet. The place was huge! They would definitely need help finding eBay.

They soon found a Search Bar run by a man called KnowsMore and it took just milliseconds for them to find the *Sugar Rush* steering wheel.

"Thank you, Mr. KnowsMore," said Vanellope, who was excited to be exploring somewhere new.

Vanellope and Ralph were quickly whisked in a pod to eBay plaza. It was a busy place of avatars and pop-up ads, but there was no time to look around. They had to hurry if they wanted to get the steering wheel in time to save Vanellope's game.

Ralph and Vanellope made it to the auction with only 31 seconds left. "We have 275," the auctioneer said. "Do I hear three?"

"Three!" Ralph called out.

He and Vanellope thought all they had to do was yell out the biggest number to win. Soon, the bidding went so high that the first bidder dropped out. But Ralph and Vanellope kept going, until...

"Sugar Rush" Steering Wheel

For vintage arcade cabinet: New condition 1999

1 bid

Seller information:
vjohnston (98★)
99% Positive feedback

Current bid: **275.00**

POWER UP

00d 00h 00m 31s

... "Sold!" said the auctioneer. "For 27,001!"

Vanellope and Ralph had won the auction! The two friends felt great until they learnt they had to pay $27,001! If they didn't pay within 24 hours, they'd lose the steering wheel.

Ralph and Vanellope went back to the pop-up ad they'd seen earlier. His name was JP Spamley. He and his partner, Gord, showed them a list of items in video games. If they could find those items, they would earn money.

A special car from *Slaughter Race* was worth even more than they needed. It belonged to Shank, the game's toughest racer.

"All's you gotta do is bring me Shank's car," said Spamley.

Ralph and Vanellope swiftly made their way to *Slaughter Race* and arrived just as two avatar players tried to take the car. But Shank and her crew knocked the players out of the game!

Ralph had an idea. He pretended to be a noise inspector to draw Shank's attention away from the car. Vanellope quickly hopped behind the wheel and hit the gas. Ralph scrambled into the car with her.

Shank wasn't about to give it up so easily. She climbed into another car and raced after Vanellope!

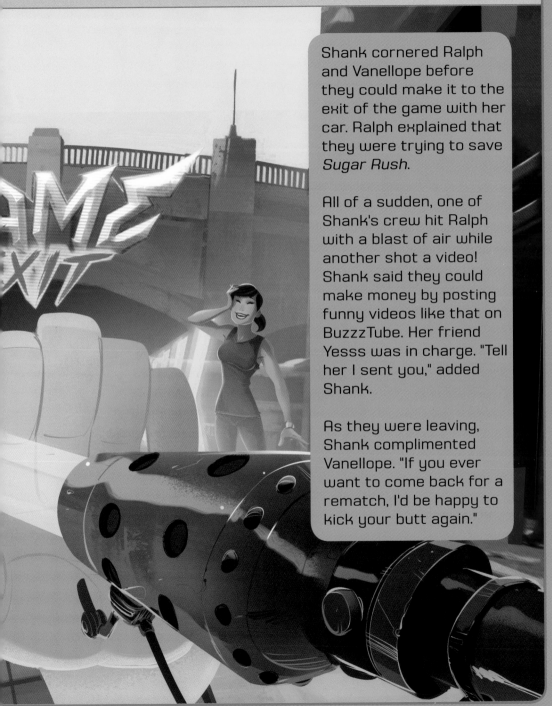

Shank cornered Ralph and Vanellope before they could make it to the exit of the game with her car. Ralph explained that they were trying to save *Sugar Rush*.

All of a sudden, one of Shank's crew hit Ralph with a blast of air while another shot a video! Shank said they could make money by posting funny videos like that on BuzzzTube. Her friend Yesss was in charge. "Tell her I sent you," added Shank.

As they were leaving, Shank complimented Vanellope. "If you ever want to come back for a rematch, I'd be happy to kick your butt again."

At BuzzzTube, Yesss loved Ralph's video. She and Ralph made even more videos, each one funnier than the last. "Oh, man. That's hilarious!" said Ralph, laughing. When Yesss put the video online, it immediately started getting hearts from viewers.

"The hearts are money, honey," said Yesss. "Every time someone gives your video a heart, you get a little cash."

...get Ralph as many hearts as possible, Yesss ordered BuzzzTube's
...ny of pop-up ads to fan out across the Internet. Vanellope volunteered
...help and went to an especially popular site – OhMyDisney.com. She
...on found herself face-to-face with the Oh My Disney princesses!

...ellope told them she was a princess, too – of *Sugar Rush*.
...ryone became good friends. The princesses loved Vanellope's
...sual fashion-sense. Before long, they were all dressed like her!
...hail Princess Vanellope, the Queen of Comfy," said Cinderella.

Having finally made enough money, Ralph was on his way to eBay. He called Vanellope to tell her he was going to pay for the wheel, and then they were going home!

After Vanellope hung up, she realised she didn't feel happy about leaving the Internet. There was just something about *Slaughter Race* that she was drawn to. It was new, exciting and unpredictable. Vanellope liked it so much, she started to sing about it.

Ralph paid for the steering wheel and contacted Vanellope again with BuzzzFace. When her phone accidentally turned on, Ralph saw that she was talking with Shank in *Slaughter Race*. Ralph was muted so Vanellope didn't know he was there as she said to Shank, "I love it here. I can't go home. I just can't."

Ralph was devastated.

Spamley heard everything Vanellope said, but he had an idea. What if they could slow *Slaughter Race* down so that Vanellope would lose interest? "Sure, great," said Ralph. "So, how do I do that?"

Spamley took Ralph to see his cousin, Double Dan. Double Dan knew how to make a virus that would slow down the game. He put the virus in a box and said to Ralph, "All you have to do is make sure the virus stays in *Slaughter Race*."

Vanellope was in the middle of a race when Ralph released the virus in *Slaughter Race*. It scanned everything, looking for weaknesses. When Vanellope glitched, the virus copied the error and spread it throughout the game!

ANNING

ANNING

INSECURITY DETECTED

Other race cars began to glitch and the track started to break apart. The game was crashing! A building collapsed and knocked Vanellope out. Ralph rushed in to rescue his friend. "C'mon Vanellope, wake up. I can't live without you," said Ralph.

Vanellope's eyes finally opened, but she didn't feel like celebrating. She blamed herself for crashing the game.

Seeing how sad his friend was, Ralph admitted he had released the virus into *Slaughter Race*. "You did this?" she asked, furiously. She threw the medal she'd made for Ralph down into the Older Net.

"I'm going back to the Internet," she announced. "Don't even think about following me." She turned and walked away.

"What have I done?" said Ralph to himself. "I ruin everything!"

Unknown to Ralph, the virus was now scanning him. "Scanning for insecurity," it said, before distributing it across the Internet...

ngry with himself, Ralph went down to the Older Net in search
f his medal. When he found it, it was broken in two. Suddenly,
omething crashed behind Ralph and he turned. A familiar looking
hadow had appeared on the wall. "Oh, no," said Ralph. "What did I do?"

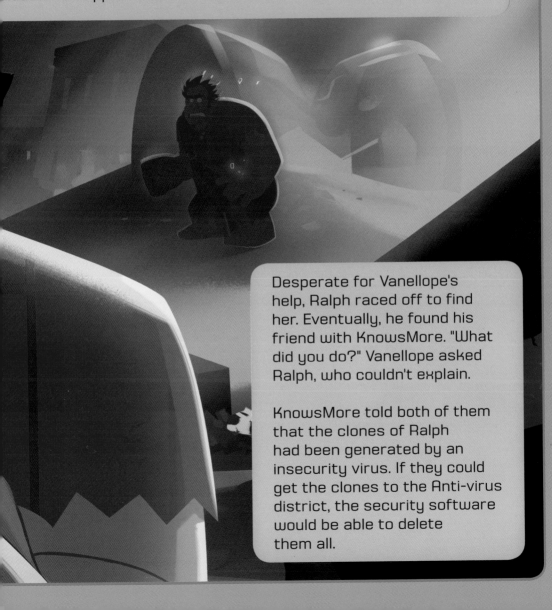

Desperate for Vanellope's
help, Ralph raced off to find
her. Eventually, he found his
friend with KnowsMore. "What
did you do?" Vanellope asked
Ralph, who couldn't explain.

KnowsMore told both of them
that the clones of Ralph
had been generated by an
insecurity virus. If they could
get the clones to the Anti-virus
district, the security software
would be able to delete
them all.

The clones all wanted one thing – Vanellope! She knew that if the clones could see her, they would follow her. She just needed a friend with some transportation and knew exactly who could help.

Once Yesss arrived with her limo, Vanellope popped out of the sunroof and teased the clones. "It's me," she shouted to the clones. "Your bestest friend in the whole wide world who you can't live without!"

The desperate clones surged towards Vanellope and bumped into the limo, sending the vehicle crashing through a skyscraper window! Everyone was okay – but not for long. Millions of clones had come together to form one gigantic Ralph clone!

The giant Ralph clone grabbed Vanellope and climbed to the top of a skyscraper. She escaped, but then it snatched Ralph and started to squeeze him. "Let him go," Vanellope pleaded, "and I'll be your best friend forever."

But Ralph said no and told the clone it couldn't stand in the way of Vanellope's dreams. "You have to let go," he added.

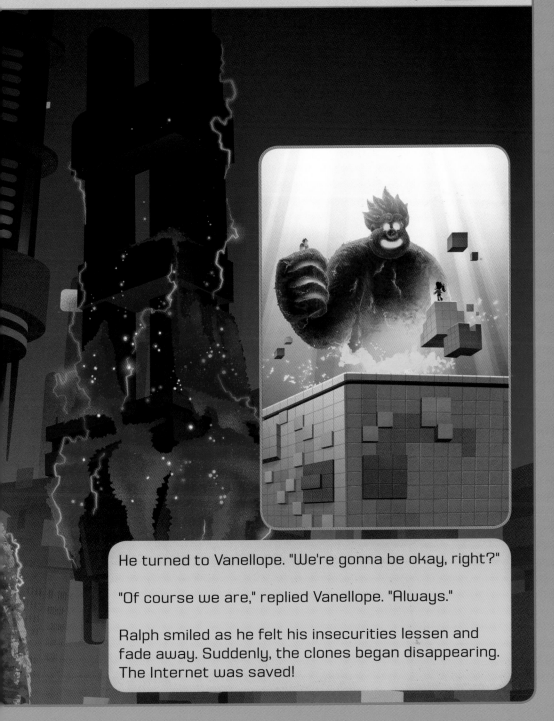

He turned to Vanellope. "We're gonna be okay, right?"

"Of course we are," replied Vanellope. "Always."

Ralph smiled as he felt his insecurities lessen and fade away. Suddenly, the clones began disappearing. The Internet was saved!

Ralph and Vanellope prepared to say goodbye, for now anyway. *Slaughter Race* was going back online and Vanellope would become part of Shank's crew. "I'll be totally safe," she told Ralph.

"I know. You'll be fine," replied Ralph, as he handed Vanellope half of his broken hero medal. "Now we can both have a half," he said.

Vanellope gave her friend a big hug. "I love you so much, you big dummy. I'm really gonna miss you."

Ralph sighed. "I'm gonna miss you, too."

Ralph was happy to be back at Litwak's with all his friends and Vanellope became one of the top racers in *Slaughter Race*. Even though they didn't spend every day together, Ralph and Vanellope remained the very best of friends.